Noddy's Special Treat

HarperCollins *Children's Books*

It was a big day in Toy Town…

Everyone was ready for the prize draw.
   Chattering excitedly, Noddy and his friends were waiting for Mr Plod the policeman to choose the winning name.

"Ladies and gentlemen," boomed Mr Plod.
"The person whose name I take out of this bowl
will win a very special treat — a train trip to the
seaside! I wonder who it will be?"

A thrill of excitement buzzed through the crowd,
and Noddy squealed, "Oh! Oh! Me! Let it be me!"

Everyone chuckled to hear Noddy so keen.

"Oh, we're all hoping to win, Noddy," said
Mrs Skittle, smiling. "Especially my little Skippy,"
she added. "He hurt his leg playing football and
missed our family trip to the seaside. So, now he
wants to go more than anything in the world."

Skippy skittled over to show Noddy his favourite book. "It's all about the things you can find at the seaside. I've read it a hundred times. If you win, you can borrow it, if you like."

"Thanks, Skippy. That's very kind," said Noddy, smiling at him.

Just then, Mr Plod took a name out of the bowl and said very loudly:

"And the winner is . . . NODDY!"

"Hurray for Noddy!" everyone cheered.

"Oh, how wonderful," cried Mrs Skittle, looking really pleased for him.

"Here's your prize, Noddy," said Mr Plod.

"Oh, wow!" Noddy gasped. "I've won TWO tickets!"

"Yes, Noddy," said Mr Plod. "You can take a friend with you. And you've got a couple of days to choose who that's going to be."

Before Noddy could even thank Mr Plod, a hand grabbed him by the shoulder.

"Whoah!" Noddy cried as he was tugged away.

"It looks as if you're going to have a problem choosing which of your friends to take with you, Noddy," he heard Mr Plod say.

"I had to get you away, Noddy," said Martha Monkey, "before one of those *selfish* people made you choose them to go with you to the seaside."

"Eh!" gasped Noddy, startled. "What do you mean, Martha? They're my friends."

"I'm your *best* friend, Noddy," Martha told him.
"Some people might pretend to be your friend –
just so they can have your other ticket."

"Hmm . . ." Noddy murmured thoughtfully.

"Best friends look after one another, Noddy.
That means they take each other to the seaside!"
Martha added.

"*Do* take me with you, Noddy," begged Martha.
"Oh, please, please! Pretty ple-e-e-ease!"

"Oh, Martha, I don't know. I need time to think about it. But, right now, I have to go!"

Noddy ran off and Martha wailed, "Wait, Noddy!" as she chased after him.

Martha Monkey couldn't find Noddy anywhere. The only person she could see was Mr Jumbo.

"Grrrr," Martha said crossly, as she raced off, "He must be here somewhere."

Noddy popped out from behind the big grey elephant. "Thanks for hiding me, Mr Jumbo!"

"Martha wants me to take her to the seaside," Noddy explained. "But I can't decide which friend to take."

"Can I give you some advice?" said Mr Jumbo.

"Oh, yes, please," said Noddy.

"Choose ME!" trumpeted Mr Jumbo. "Choose me!"

"Oh, dear," cried Noddy, and he ran off again.

Back home, Noddy found someone
working in his garden. "Martha! What are
you doing?" he asked.

"Just clearing up for you, Noddy. Best friends
help one another, remember? And they take one
another to the seaside."

"Oh," gasped Noddy.

"Ohhh," cried Noddy, as Mr Jumbo appeared, waving a paint roller in his long, grey trunk.

"Just thought I'd paint your house, Noddy."

"But Mr Jumbo – !" cried Noddy.

"No need for thanks," said Mr Jumbo. "Although, you could choose to take me to the seaside!"

"No, choose *me*!" cried Martha.

"Choose *me*!" bellowed Mr Jumbo.

The little bell on Noddy's hat tinkled as he looked first at Martha and then at Mr Jumbo as they shrieked and bellowed: "Choose ME!"

Noddy ran inside and slammed his front door.

When Martha and Mr Jumbo weren't looking, Noddy slipped out and drove to Town Square.

Almost as soon as he'd parked his car, someone opened the door for him.

"Allow me, Noddy," said Martha. "I'm sure you'll do something just as nice one day — *hint, hint* — like take me to the seaside."

"Oooh!" Noddy was dragged on to a bench.
Mr Jumbo wanted to give him some lemonade.
  "Here, have a seat. And choose *me*!" he begged.
  "No, *me*!" cried Martha. And they were off again,
shouting: "Me!" – "Me!" – "Me!" – "Me!" . . .
  "Oh, my!" groaned Noddy.

Skippy Skittle skittled up to Noddy. "You forgot
to take my seaside book, Noddy. Here, look,
I've marked the pages you might like."

"That's nice of you, Skippy, thanks," said Noddy.

"Have a good trip, Noddy," said Skippy.

Now Mr Jumbo and Martha were both trying to give Noddy a treat.

"Have this *chocolate* milkshake, Noddy," cried Martha. "And choose ME!"

"No, have this *strawberry* milkshake, and choose ME!" bellowed Mr Jumbo.

"Me!" – "Me!" – "Me!" – "Me!"

That night, poor Noddy couldn't escape from
Mr Jumbo and Martha, even in his dreams.

He tossed and turned, and he almost began
to wish he'd never won the trip to the seaside.
What a nightmare it all was!

Noddy sat up and tried singing to help him decide.

    I can't choose!
    There's no reason to pretend,
    Neither one's a better friend.
    I can't choose; it's bad news
    Trying to make up my mind.
    In the end, I find . . . I can't choose.

He couldn't stop thinking about Martha and
Mr Jumbo trying to make him choose them.

"Aghhh! Leave me alone!" he cried, leaping
out of bed. Perhaps Big-Ears could help him make
up his mind?

On the way to Toadstool House, Noddy noticed
Skippy's seaside book on the seat beside him.

It didn't take long to tell everything to Big-Ears. "They won't leave me alone," cried Noddy.

"Hmm," said Big-Ears. "So Martha and Mr Jumbo are doing you favours because they both want you to take them to the seaside?"

"But whoever I choose, the other one will be upset," cried Noddy. "What can I do?"

"You need to make up your mind, Noddy.
Then they'll stop pestering you," said Big-Ears.
"Now, who do you really want to go with?
Imagine you're at the seaside. . ."

    "OK," agreed Noddy, opening Skippy's book.
"Perhaps this will help me."

"That looks like a nice book, Noddy," said Big-Ears.
"Yes, it is. Skippy Skittle lent it to me. He was
nice to me even before I won the prize. And he
never once asked if he could—" Noddy stopped
in mid-sentence. At last, he knew what to do!
"Hey! I know who I should take!"

Mrs Skittle, Martha and Mr Jumbo all came to the station to wave goodbye to Noddy and Skippy.

"Oh, Martha. I've never seen Skippy with such a big smile," said his mother.

Martha grinned. "Yes, Noddy has made Skippy so happy I guess I'll forgive him for not taking me."

Whoo-whoo! With a jolly hoot the train started.

There was a loud sniff. It was Mr Jumbo.

"What are you crying about?" grinned Martha.
"Even I'm not that upset."

"It's not that – *sniff*. It's just that I get sad when someone nice goes away!"

"Goodbye," cried Noddy and Skippy.

"Goodbye."